For my three svelte daughters
(aka The Three Graces),
Ashley, Samantha, and Jenny
—T. J.

For Rita, Mom, and Dad,
with many thanks to Mike
—R. D.

ISBN 0-439-45948-6

Text copyright © 2004 by Roger D. Johnston and Susan T. Johnston,
as Trustees of the Johnston Family Trust.
Illustrations copyright © 2004 by Richard F. Deas.
All rights reserved. Published by Scholastic Inc.
SCHOLASTIC, CARTWHEEL BOOKS, and associated logos
are trademarks and/or registered trademarks of Scholastic Inc.

Library of Congress Cataloging-in-Publication Data is available.

10 9 8 7 6 5   05 06 07 08
Printed in the U.S.A. • First printing, October 2004

10 FAT TURKEYS

BY TONY JOHNSTON

ILLUSTRATED BY RICH DEAS

SCHOLASTIC INC.

New York Toronto London Auckland Sydney
Mexico City New Delhi Hong Kong Buenos Aires

GOBBLE GOBBLE WIBBLE WOBBLE

Do a noodle dance.

10 fat turkeys,
fooling on a fence.

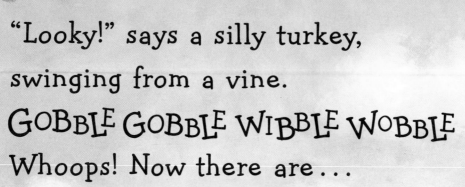

"Looky!" says a silly turkey,
swinging from a vine.
GOBBLE GOBBLE WIBBLE WOBBLE
Whoops! Now there are . . .

9 "Looky!" squawks a goofy turkey,
trying to roller-skate.
GOBBLE GOBBLE WIBBLE WOBBLE
Oops! Now there are...

8 "Looky!" calls a foofy turkey,
flapping to blue heaven.
GOBBLE GOBBLE WIBBLE WOBBLE
Oofsy! There are...

7 "Looky!" cries another turkey,
balancing some bricks.
GOBBLE GOBBLE WIBBLE WOBBLE
Uh-oh! There are...

6 "Looky!" hoots a brother turkey,
swanning a swan dive.
GOBBLE GOBBLE WIBBLE WOBBLE
Oh, no! There are...

5 "Looky!" whoops another turkey,
strutting on a boar.
GOBBLE GOBBLE WIBBLE WOBBLE
Oh, dear! There are ...

4 "Looky!" hollers out a turkey,
swallowing a bee.
GOBBLE GOBBLE WIBBLE WOBBLE
Mercy! There are...

3 "Looky!" howls a goony turkey,
whistling in a shoe.
GOBBLE GOBBLE WIBBLE WOBBLE
Ooh-ooh! There are...

2 "Looky!" shouts a loony turkey,
blowing bubble gum.
GOBBLE GOBBLE WIBBLE WOBBLE
Pop-o! Now there's...

1 "Looky!" yells the plumpest turkey,
jumping up and down.
GOBBLE GOBBLE WIBBLE WOBBLE
That's all. There are...

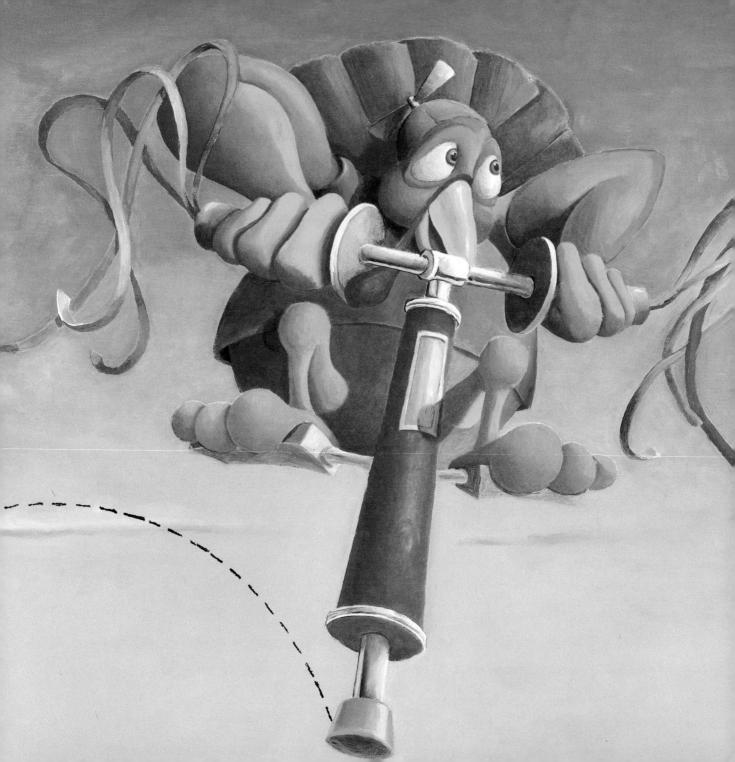

NONE!

GOBBLE GOBBLE WIBBLE WOBBLE

Do a noodle dance.

No more turkeys...

And no more fence.

Just a minute—what is this?
BIBBLE BABBLE JIBBLE JOBBLE
"Looky! Look at me!"
10 fat turkeys, fooling in a tree.

The End